Gwen 10

Editorial Director: Marge Kennedy
Retold by Janice Markham
Based on Episode #17 by Greg Klein

little monks on the wisdom tree

Ten-year-old Gwen Tennyson happily sipped her cold drink outside the gas station mini-mart while Grandpa Max filled the Rustbucket, Grandpa's trusty Recreational Vehicle (RV) with gas. She was looking forward to spending her summer vacation with Grandpa Max and her cousin Ben.

Ben seemed less excited. Even though it was already midmorning on the very first day of their adventure, he was sound asleep in the RV. But now that the Rustbucket had stopped its pleasant rocking on the road, Ben woke from his deep sleep.

"Gwen? Grandpa? Where is everyone? And where am I?" he yawned as he looked around the parking area.

Suddenly, two masked robbers ran from the mini-mart. The men knocked into Gwen, making her drop her drink.

"Hey!" Gwen protested. "That was a Super Mega Frosty..."

When Gwen saw the crooks' scary masks, however, she stopped talking and quickly hid behind the RV, dragging her half-awake cousin with her. As they crouched behind their vehicle, they could hear the rumble of the robbers' motorcycles. Then one motor died out.

"It won't start!" the crook who was holding the stolen loot shouted to his partner. As he yanked off his mask, Ben peeked out from behind the van.

"Dummy!" his partner called out, pointing to Ben. "That kid just saw you!"

Grandpa Max, meanwhile, ushered his grandchildren into the Rustbucket.

"Are you kidding me?" Ben protested. "These guys are a piece of cake. And Four Arms likes icing!" Ben said, referring to one of the aliens who could be summoned with the help of the Omnitrix. Ben couldn't understand why his grandfather was not encouraging him to catch the fleeing bandits.

He hopped out of the vehicle as he pressed on his wrist, planning to take on the bad guys.

"BEN! What are you doing, dweeb? Get in here!" Gwen shouted.

Ben ran towards the motorcycles, but Grandpa Max had gotten there first. Grandpa knocked the first robber off his bike and then slammed a trash can into the second. They fell in a heap—just in time for the police officers to take over.

"Grandpa, that was amazing back there!" Gwen exclaimed. But Ben was distracted.

"Oh, man! I can't believe this! What happened to my watch?" he said, looking around the interior of the Rustbucket.

"Ben, what're you talking about?" Gwen asked. "You don't even own a watch!"

"Is the heat getting to you?" Ben replied in exasperation. "The Omnitrix! I'm talking about the Omnitrix!"

“I’ll help you look for it,” Gwen offered. “So, uh, what does it look like?”

Ben shrieked, “YOU KNOW WHAT IT LOOKS LIKE! YOU’VE SEEN IT ALL SUMMER!”

“All summer?” Gwen asked. “Here’s a News Flash: Today is our first day of summer vacation.”

“That’s true,” Grandpa Max agreed.

“No way!” Ben argued. “Two weeks ago we were on Mount Rushmore kicking Vilgax’s butt!”

“Who’s Vilgax?” Gwen asked.

Meanwhile in outer space, the alien Vilgax's command station was in a battle with a smaller spaceship. Vilgax shouted to his second in command, "I want that ship destroyed, and I want the Omnitrix in my possession!"

Vilgax and his crew easily demolished the small spaceship. But the pod that held the Omnitrix slipped from their grasp and fell from space towards Earth.

Vilgax was furious.

"No one will control the Omnitrix but me!" he bellowed. "No one!"

"Who's Vilgax?" Ben repeated incredulously. "He's only the worst alien in the entire universe. But since he's history, we don't have to worry about him anymore."

Gwen looked at her cousin in disbelief.

"Well, that's good news," she said flatly.

Grandpa Max turned to Ben with a concerned look on his face.

"It sounds to me like this Vilgax character might be part of a science fiction movie you've seen." Gwen smiled to herself as Ben shook his head stubbornly.

"That cousin of mine has a screw loose!" she said to herself as Ben continued to search the van for the missing Omnitrix.

After a long drive, Grandpa Max finally drove the Rustbucket up to their campsite.

"We're here!" he announced to Gwen and Ben.

As soon as Ben stepped out of the RV, he figured out what was going on.

"Oh, man! I've gone back in time!" he explained to Gwen. "That's why I'm not wearing the Omnitrix yet. But I'll find it here in the woods, put it on, and ZAP, everything will be back to normal."

Gwen laughed.

"You? Normal? Yeah, right! Now if you'll excuse me, I'm headed back to the real world," she said as she started to unpack their camping equipment.

Gwen and Ben checked out the campsite while Grandpa Max worked on setting up the tent. Something wasn't quite right with the canvas shelter.

"We're short one stake," Grandpa Max finally concluded. "It must be in the back of the RV. I'll be right back."

Gwen, meanwhile, was amazed at the natural beauty around them. Suddenly, she saw a bright light streaking across the sky.

"Wow!" she exclaimed. "Ben, look at that!"

As soon as Ben looked up, the light arced and seemed to be heading straight for them.

"It's the pod! I knew it!" he said as he flew towards the landing site.

Gwen watched her cousin climb into the crater and peer into the open pod.

"The watch should be right down..." Ben began. He had no idea that Gwen had beat him to the pod by seconds. She then hid behind a bush, stifling a laugh as Ben uselessly searched the crater. Finally, she emerged with her arm straight out in front of her.

"Okay, I am ready to take this weird watch off," she announced.

Ben noticed his cousin pulling at her wrist and shrieked, "That's the Omnitrix! It's MINE!"

Gwen shrugged and said, "Finders keepers." Then, looking at it closely, she added, "And since I found it, I keep it!"

"No! I found it first," Ben barked back.

"Possession is nine-tenths of the law. Now tell me how it works, Ben!" Gwen demanded. "You seem to know all about this thing."

Ben shook his head in despair.

"No way, cuz," he sulked.

"Okay, fine," Gwen said. "I can figure this thing out on my own." Gwen pressed on the Omnitrix and quickly transformed into Heatblast! "Cool!" she called out to Ben. "I'm on fire! But I don't feel hot."

"Gwen, be careful! You could start a forest fire," Ben warned.

In an instant, Gwen sent fireballs into the air that spelled out the word "G W E N."

"Whoa!" Ben exclaimed. "It took me like a month to learn how to do that when I was Heatblast!"

"This is GREAT!" Heatblast-Gwen said to her cousin as she continued to experiment with Heatblast's powers. Then she turned to Ben and asked, "Can the watch turn me into anyone else?"

"This could be fun," Ben thought. He fidgeted with the Omnitrix and transformed Gwen into the miniature alien Greymatter! Suddenly, a large raccoon approached. It looked hungrily at the little alien.

Greymatter-Gwen gasped and squeaked out, "Ben! This isn't funny!"

"It's funny to me!" Ben laughed as he picked up his puny cousin and asked, "So who's got this alien stuff down now?"

Just then, a robot drone landed nearby.

"Let's go!" Ben urged. "Those campers are gonna need help."

Back at the campsite, the enormous robot drone blew away tables, tents and picnic items, all in search of the Omnitrix. People fled in every direction. By the time Ben and Gwen got to the campsite, Gwen had become Diamondhead, and the drone was holding a park ranger in its powerful metal pincers.

"Hey!" shouted Diamondhead-Gwen. "Leave him alone!"

The drone dropped the park ranger and fired at Gwen. The force of the weapon knocked her down.

Suddenly, Grandpa Max came up the hill, carrying an armful of firewood, along with the missing tent stake.

"Ben, what's going on? And where's Gwen?" he asked, gesturing nervously to the alien Diamondhead.

"Grandpa, it's me. Gwen!" the crystalline heroine answered.

Grandpa Max was stunned, but, seeing the drones descend on the campsite, he had no time to consider the situation.

"Ben, come on!" he urged. "Help me get everyone out of here!"

The lead drone approached Diamondhead-Gwen again. As Gwen raised her alien arm, metal projectiles fired out, piercing the invader.

"Cool! This thing lets me shoot daggers!" Gwen cheered as she sent forth a torrent of spikes. "Take THAT, robot!" she shouted.

Grandpa Max and Ben peered out from behind the Rustbucket.

"Whoa! She's good," Grandpa Max said.

"So was I!" Ben complained. "I'm supposed to be the hero!"

Diamondhead-Gwen's blast did not stop the robot drone. It blasted her with a powerful laser. Using her gem-like contours, she refracted the laser blast, sending it back on her attacker. The powerful light beam destroyed the drone.

Up in his giant spaceship, Vilgax was furious.

"My drones are all destroyed! Whoever has the Omnitrix possesses great power," Vilgax observed. "Now he–or she–will have to deal with me!"

Then next morning, Ben stepped out of the tent, yawning deeply. He found his cousin standing outside.

"When did you get up?" he asked.

Gwen smiled and said, "I never went to bed. First I was a high-tech alien, and I merged with my laptop to triple its processing speed. And then I turned into this water creature to catch us some lunch." She showed him the large fish she had caught. "Next, I became this speed-freak alien, so I decided to go home and pick up these clothes that I'd forgotten to pack."

"The Omnitrix is a complicated piece of alien technology," Ben said. "It's not about having fun."

"Wanna bet? Follow me. Unless you're afraid..." Gwen said, knowing that Ben wouldn't be able to resist a challenge.

"I'm not afraid of anything," Ben said.

Gwen, as XLR8, whisked Ben to a bowling alley that she had found not far from their campsite. Normally, Ben liked bowling. However, when he looked over at his cousin and saw that she had now transformed herself into Four Arms-Gwen, he felt a little out of his league.

"Strike!" Gwen's alien-self called out after each frame, while Ben rolled gutter balls.

"This isn't fair!" said Ben admitting, "I don't like seeing that you're better with it than I was."

Suddenly a huge spiky ball crashed through the bowling alley.

"Uh, oh!" Ben gasped. "He's not supposed to be here."

"What's going on?" Four Arms-Gwen asked.

"It's VILGAX!" Ben cried as Gwen's ten-minute time limit expired, and she transformed back into herself.

"Who should I become?" she shouted as she pounded on the Omnitrix, trying to get it to reactivate. Panicking, she pleaded, "Ben, it's not working! Help me!"

"It's got to recharge," Ben explained as Vilgax emerged from the spiky ball.

Vilgax charged over to Gwen.

"Give me the Omnitrix! Now!" he demanded. But it would not come off Gwen's wrist. He pressed down on the device with a mix of discouragement and determination.

"I can't remove it here. But that should stop it from activating for a while," Vilgax growled.

Gwen looked up at Vilgax bravely.

"You wouldn't hurt a girl, would you?" she asked.

"Hurt you? No. I have something much worse in mind for you," Vilgax sneered. He grabbed Gwen by the arm and fled the scene.

Grandpa Max drove up and shouted, "Get in!" to Ben.

"Gr-Grandpa!" Ben stammered. "Okay, you've got to believe me on this. Vilgax is here and..."

Grandpa nodded, "...he wants the Omnitrix so he took Gwen."

"How did you know?" Ben asked.

Grandpa Max revealed the secret technology that was housed in the dashboard of the Rustbucket: "In-dash intergalactic monitoring system. Went haywire about a half hour ago. His ship must be due west of here." He then paused and looked straight at Ben. "Since you've lived this before, what's Vilgax going to do with Gwen?" he asked.

"Let's just say you better floor it," Ben replied.

Inside the spaceship, Vilgax was getting ready to take possession of the Omnitrix once and for all. He placed Gwen on an operating table, holding her there with metal restraints. As he commanded his robots to prepare for takeoff, he reached into a bag of sharp tools. Gwen tried to reason with him.

"Can't you just slip the watch off my wrist?" she suggested.

Just then, the Rustbucket rammed into the spaceship, and Grandpa Max jumped out, holding a weapon that Ben had never seen before.

"Get your claws off my granddaughter, Vilgax!" he demanded.

"Tennyson!" Vilgax shouted, as if welcoming an old friend. Then he added, "You'll never destroy me, you worthless human!" Vilgax shot a blast from his laser at Grandpa Max while he grabbed for the Omnitrix. But when Grandpa Max fell, Ben grabbed his weapon and attacked the evil alien. As the battle continued, the Omnitrix snapped off Gwen's wrist and flew onto Grandpa Max's arm.

"*NO!*" Vilgax screamed.

"*NO!*" echoed Ben. "I was supposed to get it!"

There were just seconds to spare before Vilgax's ship blasted off with the Tennysons trapped inside.

"You gotta go Upgrade, Grandpa! Trust me!" Ben shouted, quickly programming the Omnitrix on Grandpa's wrist.

In a flash, Grandpa Max-Upgrade flung Vilgax aside and hit a switch to destroy Vilgax's ship. As the countdown began, he grabbed Ben and Gwen and jumped into the Rustbucket. Back on land, as Vilgax's ship exploded above them, Grandpa Max became himself again. But there was one more thing that needed to get done.

Gwen snapped the Omnitrix off Grandpa Max and placed it firmly on Ben's wrist.

"Hey, how did you do that?" Ben asked.

Gwen smiled. "I'll never tell."